D0960819

MY AMERICA

Our Strange New Land

Elizabeth's Diary

by Patricia Hermes

Scholastic Inc. New York

Jamestown, Virginia
1609

August 11, 1609

Today, we came to land at last! It seems there are no bones in my legs. I hugged my friend Jessie. We held each other up. Still, the land seemed to bob around beneath us. Seventy-one days. That is how long we were on the ocean.

Nine ships sailed from Plymouth, England. But at sea, a hurricane struck. Oh, how it struck! It became blacker than night. The waves brought us up into the dark sky, and then slammed us down. Men were washed off deck and into the sea. Some men tied themselves to the mast. But then — the mast broke off. Our ship rolled and rats came out. I tried to hold back tears, but could not. Jessie cried, too. Mama said we should not show fear or dismay. But soon, she cried, too. Prayers flew up to heaven like little birds. After the storm, when it became quiet, we looked about. Then, even Papa had tears in his eyes. For five of our ships were gone. One missing ship is the *Sea Venture*. It held our food! Were the ships blown off course? Or are they at the bottom of the ocean? We do not know.

Still, we are safely in Jamestown. I am here with my mama and papa. Soon, our new baby will be born. But it will be a home without Caleb, my twin. He stayed behind with Mama's cousin because his lungs are weak. He will join us come spring. I pray that spring comes soon, because without Caleb it will be a sad home.

August 11, later

It is *hot* inside this fort where we shall live for a while. Nothing stirs but nasty mosquitoes. They bite and sting. They get in my ears. Jessie and I compete for who can swat the most. I have killed twenty-seven. Jessie is winning, for she has slain thirty. Mama rubs fennel into the bites. Already, though, my neck is as fat as a melon.

Papa says that tomorrow we shall begin to build our house. He says there will be no bugs inside our house. Captain Gabriel Archer was one of those in charge of our expedition. He has lived here before. He says, "You wait and see. There are always bugs."

Gabriel Archer is a dreadful, unpleasant man.

August 11, again

I close this book. I open this book. I fear I shall use it up in one day! But there is much to write about here. Like this: To cool off, Jessie and I splashed in the river. I fell down in the water. A fat, silver fish swam right into my lap! It was as big around as a newborn pig. I squealed and laughed. Mama did not stop our play though our skirts poured water. I think she is happy that we run free. For now. But soon we shall begin to work.

Also today, I met Captain John Smith, the leader here. He is jolly and has wild ginger hair. It flies about his head as he races around camp. He shouted a greeting to me. He called me "Lizzy." I believe I shall like Captain Smith.

August 11, yet again!

I know I am going to use up this book and all my ink in just one day. But I must write this. Today, oh joy! I met an Indian, two Indians, three, and even more! We have heard much about them. And now I have seen them with my very own two eyes.

This is what happened: An Indian came to me. He bent close and looked right into my face. He smelled like fish and smoky fires. And oh, guess what? He was almost naked! I could not help it. I covered my eyes and turned away. But Papa said, "Elizabeth! Daughter!"

I quick took my hands away. Then, the Indian put his two golden hands on my head. He touched my cap. And he smiled at me. He spoke some words, but what, I cannot say.

I believe that what he said was gentle. For his face was kind.

Oh, to think that I have truly met an Indian! To think that I am in Jamestown. I am not on a ship! To think that we are here at last!

August 11, darkness falls

I talk too much. I talk too fast. I even walk too fast. Mama scolds. She tells me, Elizabeth Barker, do not babble. Be proper.

Papa does not scold. He just smiles and calls me by his pet name. He says, Sweet Beth, try to go slowly.

I do try. But it is hard to be proper. It is also no fun at all. This evening, I raced Jessie to the well.

She pushed a little.

I pushed a little.

She pushed more.

I pushed more.

And I tumbled and fell headlong into a

pricker bush. Mama spent much time pulling prickers out of me. I spent much time trying not to cry. Jessie held my hand. Mama again told me to go slow! Be proper, Elizabeth! I think I hear those words in my sleep.

I promise to go slow. I shall try to be proper. And I shall try not to babble. I shall write clearly. But tonight, I am tired. And sore from prickers! I shall write more tomorrow.

August 12, 1609, morning

Last night, we returned to the ship to sleep. This morning, we are back on land. This is what I see from where I sit. Before me is a clearing, shaped like a triangle. Around it is a palisade, a tall wooden fence. Inside the fence is a church and a well. There is a large storehouse for food. There are thatched houses, with pine trees all around. But there is no schoolhouse —

not yet. Papa says perhaps someday there will be. And in this New World, he says, perhaps girls may attend school! In England, only boys go to school, which I think unfair.

The fence has two gates. One faces the James River. The other opens to the woods. The woods are dark and thick with pine trees. The wind sighs in the treetops. It makes a rushing sound. It makes me think of the ocean. Small bugs and creatures hum in the grass. I hear birds calling and twittering. Last night, I heard an owl. It seemed to ask my name. Who, who, it called, who, who?

It is a strange land. But it is very, very beautiful.

August 12, later

I must tell why we are in the New World. We came to seek gold and rich things. Those will be sent back to the Virginia Company in England.

Papa and Mama do not want rich things for themselves. They want only land. In England, Papa paid much to rent land. Here, he can own land. He can *be* a landowner. That is what we will work for in Jamestown.

I do not mind working for land with Mama and Papa here.

But secretly, I would like to have gold and some fine, rich things, too.

August 13, 1609

I am writing in this book for Caleb. I will tell him all we see and do.

And now I must tell of a troublesome thing. This journal where I write is Caleb's drawing book. The night before we sailed, I hid it in my trunk. I meant to ask Caleb if I might take it. But I forgot. No, that is not true. I did not forget. If I write here, I will be truthful. I learned to read and write at home. I wished to write about our journey. Yet, I knew 'twas wrong, and went to give it back. But in the morning — the trunk was gone! It had been moved onto the ship.

I pray that Caleb will get a new drawing book.

August 13, later

I must tell about Jessie Bolton, my new friend. I did not know her in England. We met on board our ship. We are much the same. She is nine years old, like me. She has yellow hair and blue eyes. Like me. She was born in October. Like me. She has freckles. Like me. We are the exact same height.

But Jessie is fair to look on. I believe I am

rather plain. And we are different inside. Jessie is thoughtful. She does not babble. And she has a prayerful mind.

I am sometimes careless. And though I mean to pray, I do forget at times.

But I do not talk back to any elders. And Jessie does. She even talks back to Gabriel Archer. And oh, how she can mimic him! He puffs out his cheeks when he talks. He looks like a big fish. Jessie goes behind his back and makes faces. I think I will burst when she does that.

Jessie and I have made a plan. When there is no one looking, we shall shed our hot English clothes. Already, today, we shed shoes and stockings.

I told Jessie that we must also shed our petticoats and shifts. She laughed and said that then we might look like the Indians!

Imagine wearing so little! But we did not

shed our shifts or linen skirts. It would be too improper.

Sometimes Jessie is sad, though. Her mother is very ill. We are afraid. For crossing the ocean, we saw many die.

August 14, 1609

Good news! Today, we shall begin to build our house. Jessie's papa will build a house beside ours! And this I do not like — the mean Bridger boys will have their house on the other side. The Bridger boys make it their life's work to torment Jessie and me. John Bridger is the worst, worse than James and even little Thomas.

Today, John saw me writing. He snatched my journal and held it behind his back. And believe this — I did kick John Bridger to get back my book. How dare he try to read my secret thoughts!

I snatched it and hid it in my skirts.

When I heard about the Bridgers' house, I ran to Papa. I said I did not want the mean Bridger boys next to us. Must they be our neighbors?

Papa laid a hand on my head. He smiled at me. He said I must remember this: We are all neighbors here.

August 15, 1609

The men who were here before us make a fuss over us children. Those men came here two years past, but they brought no children. Our ships brought seventeen boys and seven girls. Jessie and I are the youngest girls. I wish Caleb were among the boys!

Mr. Foster, a thin, ragged man, has been here two years. His eyes were sad when he saw Jessie and me. He said he has children in England. He misses them sorely.

I felt dreadful sad. We brought mail on our ship. But there was no letter for him. Still, in the storm, many things and people were tossed into the sea. Perhaps his letter was among the lost.

I shall try to be a friend to Mr. Foster.

August 16, 1609

I have a puzzle, and it is this: I know now why there is a fence. It is to keep out the Indian warriors. Mr. Archer says that at night they creep silently to scale the walls. He calls them treacherous, thieving rascals.

Yet, I have met these Indian men. They were kind. And now, in this morning light, they are all around. They are helping with corn. They taught the English men to plant. They taught the men to fish and hunt.

And the Indian patted my head and smiled at me.

So here is more of the puzzle: Captain Smith says the Indians are good, but they do attack. Only, he says, because the men here treat them badly.

So how do I understand this puzzle? I cannot. If Caleb were here, he would talk about this. Together, we would understand.

August 17, 1609

I must tell about Gabriel Archer, though it pains me just to say his name. He is rude and thinks he should rule all! Still, he is an important man. He says he had a letter from the Virginia Company. That letter told that

Captain Smith was no longer the leader here. It said others should be leaders. The letter though was on the *Sea Venture*, lost in the hurricane along with some of the newly appointed leaders. So we do not know if he tells the truth.

Most of the men want Captain Smith as their leader. But some choose one of the men named George Percy. And some choose Mr. Archer. I asked Jessie, "Why choose a big fish for a leader?"

Mama heard and scolded me. But I only spoke the truth.

Sometimes I have this thought. I pretend that Gabriel Archer was swept away in the hurricane. But then I tell God that I do not really *wish* that. It is just a thought. And thoughts sometimes come unbidden. They just run around like little mice inside my head.

August 18, 1609

Today, Papa sent Jessie and me to the woods to gather reeds. We shall use them to thatch our roofs. Mama told us to look for herbs, too, especially what is called snakeroot here in Virginia. Many here are ill with fever.

Many are healthy, though. Yet some refuse to work. They say they are gentlemen and need servants.

Papa thinks they are very foolish. He smiled at Jessie and me when we brought home the reeds. He said he is proud that we work so hard to build our homes.

I smiled back at him. One cannot help but smile when Papa smiles. But today I am sad. This does not feel like home. Home is England. Home is where Caleb is. What is he doing now? I wonder. Has he found a checkers partner? We played together and, mostly, I won! Does he know I took his book?

Does he still cough?

I wonder if he misses me.

August 18, night

When it is night, I miss my twin brother most. When Mama and Papa were planning our journey, Caleb and I lay awake, listening. We heard that Caleb might stay behind because of his lungs! I told Caleb: If a cough is coming, run outside. Even if it is cold, run so no one will hear. He did. But then in his sleep, he coughed and gasped even more. Mama and Papa would hurry in. I was afraid. Did he cough more because he ran outside?

August 19, 1609

Some things are good here. And some are very bad.

This is today's list:

Good: Jessie's mama took some broth.

Bad: I had porridge for breakfast. And dinner. And supper.

Good: Our house is rising.

Bad: The Bridgers' house has posts raised too.

I shall end with a good thing: Mama is happy. She says Jamestown begins to feel like home.

August 20, 1609

I despise John Bridger! Jessie and I go to hidden places so I can write in this book. But John Bridger does sneak and follow us. Tonight, he says he will tell Mama that I write secretly.

I do not want Mama to know, for what shall I say? Shall I say that Caleb *gave* me this book? I do not want to lie to Mama. But I lied to John. I said I was writing a poem for Mama. I do not think he believed me. He waddled off, laughing. He sways when he walks, just like a hog.

He is certainly not handsome!

August 20, later

A secret to tell. Though it was crowded on our ship, room was found for eight horses. Here, the horses stay within a fenced pasture. Jessie and I sit on the fence and talk to them. Charlie is our favorite. He frolics like a child. I think it is because he has been cooped up for so long. A ship is as hard on a horse, says Papa, as it is on a child.

Today, as we sat on the fence, I saw that no

one was about. I smiled at Jessie. Then I leapt from the fence onto Charlie's back.

And then do you know? Jessie leapt up behind me. For a moment, Charlie galloped like the wind. I hung on to his mane. Jessie hung on to me. It was a wonderful moment. Till we both fell off.

Tonight, I cannot tell Mama why it is that I cannot sit on my bottom.

August 21, 1609

Today, Jessie and I again went outside the palisade gates. We searched for herbs and berries, for food is scarce here.

The day was hot, and after a bit, we waded in the river. I made up a water song. I sang: Plash! My feet have a bath.

Jessie made up a food song: We eat our porridge. It tastes so horrid!

We laughed as we gathered up the reeds.

After a time, though, we became quiet. Birds flitted by, singing their songs. These birds are not gray like English sparrows. Some are brilliant blue and some are yellow. Some are red with crests on their heads. Even the black birds are not dull black. We saw a black bird with red and yellow stripes on its wing. It sang sweetly, clinging to the side of a reed. Jessie and I listened and maybe forgot our task. But just for a little while. For it is strange here. It is not home like England.

But it is a sweet and beautiful land.

August 22, 1609

Today, Jessie and I were gathering reeds. We had shed our shoes and stockings. Suddenly, at the river, Jessie grabbed my hand. A funny brown-and-black monkey ran past us! It had a sweet face and a small black mask. It stopped and watched us, not at all afraid. It dipped its paws in the water. Then it ate something from its paws. I do believe the monkey had caught a fish.

Who ever heard of a fish-eating monkey?

I could not wait to tell my papa.

August 22, later

I am in disgrace. I lost my shoes in the forest. I was so excited to see the monkey — and it was *not* even a monkey! It was a raccoon, I have learned. In my hurry to tell Papa, I forgot my shoes. For hours I searched for them. Jessie came with me, for she forgot her shoes, too.

Mama scolded me. She asked where I thought I might get another pair!

I will be content with Indian moccasins all winter! That is what I said inside my head. For

I was feeling rebellious. And ashamed of myself. But I did not speak those words.

I have never seen Mama more angry.

Papa was not angry. He was just quiet. Still, I know that he was disappointed.

I am disappointed in myself.

August 22, night

My shoes are still missing. And Mama is still cross. She scolded me again at supper. She said I was foolish and careless.

I know I deserved the scolding. I *was* foolish and I *was* careless. But I think there is another reason Mama is angry. There is much disease and illness here. I think she worries for the baby. She worries for Jessie's mama, too. She still lies on her pallet, pale and silent.

I wonder if Mama knows about this book. She frowns at me when I open my chest where

I keep my things. Does she know I took Caleb's drawing book? Perhaps she knows I am not only a foolish child, but a thieving child besides.

August 23, 1609, such news!

This afternoon, two more ships from our fleet arrived! They were *not* at the bottom of the ocean. They were blown far off course in the hurricane. And here they came upriver! Oh, it was such a sight. We watched them come, their white sails billowing in the wind. Jessie and I raced to the riverbank to greet them. The people who came off ship looked ill. Some were pale and ghostly-looking. For they are very hungry. And they have no news of the ship, the *Sea Venture*. We have great need of that ship, for it holds so many men and much-needed supplies.

We helped them to unload. And oh, Jessie and I rejoiced. Because new children have arrived! There are no boys, but there are little twin girls, Sarah and Abigail. There is also another girl of nine years named Claire. She ducks her head as though she is shy. But she smiles sweetly and her eyes twinkle. I think that I will like her.

The church bells toll, and we thank God for their deliverance.

Secretly, I thank God there are no more boys like the Bridger boys.

August 24, 1609

Mistress Bolton becomes more ill. Today, Jessie stayed by her side.

And I have again spent the day searching for our shoes. And promising myself that I will no longer be a foolish child.

August 24, late

I have found our shoes! And our stockings. They were on the rock where we left them. But they were hidden by vines, which seem to grow a yard a minute! They smell dreadful, for things rot quickly here. But I rubbed them with salt. Then I laid them in the sun to dry. I think they will be fine to wear again. Mama smiled at me this morning. When she brushed my hair, her hand was gentle. I think she has forgiven me. This time.

I wish I could forgive myself so easily. This book feels heavy in my hand at times.

August 25, 1609

Something good! Today, our papas raised the forks to support our roofs. Now they are adding upright timbers for the walls. But they need someone to scamper up the roof to do the thatch.

I have become strong and agile. So I quickly offered to do it.

Papa agreed.

But Mama said no.

I begged.

Mama refused.

I begged more.

Mama refused more. She said it was work for a boy.

She turned her back then, but I saw a tear. I thought I knew why she cried.

I took her hand. I told her that Caleb will be here, come spring. I told her that I want to help. I promised to tie my skirt so to appear like breeches. For I know Mama wants me to be proper.

She said then that I might do it. But her eyes were still sad.

Poor Mama, she acts so brave. But I believe she misses England and English ways. I know she misses Caleb. We all do.

August 25, later

Our house is rising fast! The sides are up, and now I start to thatch the roof.

Captain Smith came by and called up to me. He told me that I put many men to shame with my hard work.

And then, do you know? He climbed right on the beams to work beside me. He spoke to me as though I were a grown person. He said many men here do not want to work. They think that they are gentlemen. They want everyone to be their servants and slaves. I have seen that myself. The men stand by the well, fanning themselves. Some lie on the riverbank. Some sleep all through the hot afternoons. They order the Indians to do their work.

Well. I told him what I thought. I said that if these men do not work, they should not eat! Food is hard to come by here.

Captain Smith laughed. He says I should help him govern. Imagine that! I believe I would enjoy that. I would tell people what to do. I would send John Bridger to work in the hottest field. And in the hottest part of the day. And I would make Gabriel Archer work with him. And I would allow my papa to rest. He looks tired now.

Captain Smith looked worried, though. Papa is worried, too, I know. I think Papa is also disappointed. We came for land. But this land is filled with sickness and hunger and danger. It is a vastly different land from what we had been told.

August 25, later

Papa sent me to lie under a tree to rest. He said I look flushed and ill. I know he fears the summer sickness. But I am not ill. I am only hot!

It *is* hot work thatching the roof. Yet although I would not say it to Mama, I like it better than mending stockings!

Still, Papa said I must lie in the shade.

And so I lay and watched the boys working. I thought about Caleb. If he were here, he would work hard. And maybe with the sun and heat, he would not cough. Oh, and if he were here, he would make pictures. He would draw portraits of Jessie and the Indians. He would sketch this whole entire town. I believe he would put in all the details — birds, and even mice and voles. He might even draw the cricks and cracks in the wooden fence. And oh, I cannot wait till he sees the raccoons! What a portrait he will make of them.

But I have his drawing book.

That still troubles my heart.

August 25, nighttime

Tonight, I think about girls and boys and other strange things. Today, as I lay resting, I saw Mary Dobson and John Bridger talking together. John came and sat by Mary's side. They sat very close. Very close!

John Bridger is not a bit handsome. And still, Mary blinked her eyes at him and smiled.

They thought I did not see. But I did. For a moment, John Bridger lay his hand over Mary's hand. For fifteen seconds it lay there. I counted each second.

Imagine holding the hand of John Bridger. It makes chills go up and down my spine.

August 26, 1609

Today, we had a picnic. We brought food and drink to share. That was Captain John Smith's idea. He worries about the strife here. He wants us all to be one big family. But that is hard with so many who will not work.

Before our picnic, Papa took me, Jessie, and my new friend, Claire, to gather food. We dug in the river for clams. Suddenly, an Indian came silently from the woods. He stood right by me in the river. At first, I was afraid. My heart did knock and thump. But Papa nodded that it was all right. And then the Indian man took my hand. He gave me a forked stick. He showed me how to dig a crab. It takes patience and a slow motion. I was very patient and very slow. And I caught one! It was large with fierce claws. I dangled it in Jessie's face. She squealed. Then, the Indian scooped up a fish with his bare hands. He handed it to Claire. She jumped back and waved him away. The fish flopped itself into the waters.

Then, the Indian jumped backward. He wiggled his hands before his face. He pretended to be Claire and to be afraid. We all laughed. Even the Indian laughed. Only Claire did not laugh. She ducked her head and twisted her hands beneath her apron.

I told her we did not mean to tease.

August 27, 1609, night

It was so hot today, even my teeth felt hot. Tonight, a small breeze blows and cools us some. I wonder if it is hot where Caleb is this night.

Papa misses Caleb dearly. When he speaks of Caleb, his eyes get sad like Mama's do. Yet I wonder if either Mama or Papa miss him as I do. I think it is because we are twins. We twins know each other's hearts. And thoughts.

Now, I have a new fear. I fear that in this long year apart Caleb will forget me. So this is what I do — at night, I send him thoughts. I picture them as tiny birds. They fly to Caleb and make him think of me.

If those bird-thoughts flew to Mama tonight, I know just what she would say. She would say again — you are a foolish child.

August 28, 1609

Mistress Bolton has eaten nothing for three whole days. Each day, we fear that she will die. Jessie has become most quiet.

Mr. Bolton has taken to talking loudly to his

poor, sick wife. He tells her all he's seen and done each day. But she can no longer hear him. So he talks louder until Papa leads him away to rest.

One of the women who came last week has died. Her name was Mistress Pickett. She died in childbirth. Her baby boy lived for just a few hours.

I feel sad inside. I am sad for Mistress Pickett. But I am more sad for her tiny baby. It seems dreadful to be newly born, and then to die so quickly.

Tonight, I remembered to pray. I prayed for Jessie and her mama and her papa. I prayed for Mistress Pickett and for her poor dead baby.

I prayed for Mama and our baby.

August 29, 1609

An Indian girl came to our town! She is perhaps thirteen years old. They call her Pocahontas. Her father is the chief called Powhatan. She has smooth skin and black eyes and thick black hair. She is lively and ever so funny!

When she came to the clearing, she stared at Jessie and me. Then she ran to me and tipped back my cap. She touched my hair. She said, "Look! 'Tis gold!"

I could not have been more surprised had a blackbird spoken to me. She spoke in English!

I laughed. I said, "Not gold, yellow."

And then, oh this is hard to believe, but it is true. She climbed a tree. She clapped her hands. "Come!" she said. "Climb up with me."

I looked at Jessie. She looked at me.

Oh, I wanted to climb that tree. But I wore a skirt and petticoats. I thought of what I had said — that we should dress as Indians do. Perhaps someday. But today, we had to shake our heads. We told Pocahontas, no. We could not climb that tree.

August 29, later

I must tell more about Pocahontas. She is sweet and kind. She is also very, very good. She is a dear friend of Captain Smith.

Her father, Chief Powhatan, once captured Captain Smith. The chief believed Captain Smith meant to harm his people. And so, it is said, the chief meant to kill Captain Smith. Captain Smith was held down, his head against a rock. The warriors were about to club him to death. Imagine that! The thought of it makes me weak and shivery. But Pocahontas, her father's favorite daughter, sought to spare Captain Smith's life. Since then, she goes between us and her people, keeping peace. Captain Smith learns the Indians' language from her. And this is how she learned our language. Each time she comes, she brings gifts.

Today, she came with a gift bearer. His name is Rawhunt, and he is a small, twisted man. He carried gifts for us, things we need so badly. There was corn and two large fish in a beautiful woven basket.

It was a gift, a sign, said Captain Smith, that the Indians wish us well.

Gabriel Archer said not to trust such signs.

Sometimes, I become weary of Gabriel Archer.

August 30, 1609

Here is the newest mean thing John Bridger did. I was on the rooftop, working with thatch.

It cuts your hands and makes them raw. A reed slipped from my sore hands. It fairly flew into the space between the Bridgers' house and ours.

John Bridger stood there looking up. Of course, he was not working — just looking. And he shouted at me to come down. He said I was a foolish girl and had no business on the roof.

I told him he should come up then and work. But then I said no. If he did, the roof would break, for he is as big around as a hog. I said that right out loud.

Just as Mama passed below.

And now I am in disgrace. Again.

August 30, later

Mama has not stayed angry for long this time. I think she, too, is not fond of the

Bridger family. Mr. Bridger does little work. After weeks here, their house has just a few posts raised. And when he does work, he begs! He begs nails from Papa, things he should have brought himself. And Papa is too kind to refuse. Then, Mama becomes angry. They are all lazy, and do not work for the common good, even the mother. Today, we women and girls went to the river to wash clothing. Mrs. Bridger came, too. Like her son, she waddles. She was breathless and sweating. At the riverbank, she did no work! She sat on a rock, her smelly feet in the river. She fanned herself with a leaf. She sighed about the heat and bugs. And then — believe this! — she ordered Jessie to wet a cloth and bathe her neck.

Jessie did it, but her face was set with anger. If it were me, I'd wish for the courage to put a viper inside that wet cloth.

I turned to Mama. I whispered that in

England, the Bridger family would not be our friends.

Mama tightened her mouth. She looked away. After a moment, she said this: We are not in England now.

August 31, 1609

There are others here as ill as Mistress Bolton. Some call it the summer sickness. It comes on quickly. The body burns with fever. There are deliriums. Many times death comes in just two days.

The medicine kit that Mama brought is near empty. There is only aqua vitae. That must be used sparingly. It can make a person wild in the head. Also, herbs that Mama brought to plant are not flowering in this dry heat. We look in the forest and field for feverwort and Virginia snakeroot and everlasting. We work and we pray. And when we can, we play. It is hard now for Jessie to laugh and play.

September 1, 1609, a new month

Papa says this month will be better than last. He counted our blessings at prayer time last evening. He said, "Six ships have made the crossing safely. We have food to eat and work to do. Mrs. Bolton is no worse. Soon, our house will be built. Let us be thankful."

It is odd, perhaps, to count Jessie's mama as a blessing. But we have seen the sickness kill quickly. Many more of the new people have died. We have a burial most every night now. But our hopes are raised, for Mistress Bolton clings to life.

And when Papa came to tell me sweet dreams last night, he called me Sweet Beth.

He also told me a secret. He brought a card of pins from England and a pincushion. He has hidden it from Mama. And now, if I will make a design of pins, we will give this gift to Mama when our baby is born. I might spell out a welcome with pins. What shall I write? *Welcome, little stranger?* I am so happy at the thought.

September 1, later

Today, Captain Smith declared a holiday for the children. We went outside the fence to play. Jessie and I swung from the vines that hang from the trees. The bigger girls watched us play. They did not join us. They pretend to be too old. But they did play with the hoop toy that Claire brought from England. Mary Dobson sat on a rock with her skirts spread about her. She squealed if anyone stirred up dust. I am afraid that I did deliberately cast a bit of mud onto her feet. It seemed almost like an England summer day.

Until John Bridger spoiled it all. He flung a fat yellow frog at me. It landed with a dull thump on my bare feet.

Jessie and I fled.

We did not scream, though. And we did not tell our papas. Instead, I plan revenge.

September 1, nighttime

In the forest, I found a fat dead snake. It was horrid and smelled bad. I picked it up, though I felt squeamish. I hid it beneath my skirts. I called Jessie to me and showed her. We went behind the well where the weeds are tall. It was almost dark, and no one was about. Jessie acted as lookout. I hid the snake in the weeds.

That is how we plot our revenge.

September 2, 1609

We always know when the Bridger family is asleep. That is because Mr. Bridger makes horrible, whistling snores. Tonight, when they are asleep, I will do it.

By moonlight, September 3, 1609, about midnight

The fat black snake is there. I left it curled beside John Bridger's face.

September 3, morning

We woke to shouts and yelps. Big, brave John Bridger was howling.

I laughed and buried my face in the pillow.

Later, I told him sweetly that black snakes are poisonous.

He squinted up his eyes at me. He asked how came it there.

I smiled.

September 3, night

Some things I do not understand. Like this: The men here learned many things from the Indians. They learned to plant corn. They learned to fish. They learned to lay traps for deer. They learned to make canoes from hollowed-out logs. But the Indians frighten us, too. They carry bows and arrows. There are tales told of how they attack at night. Some nights, I wake shaking with bad dreams.

And we know that they *do* attack at times. Captain Smith says they attack sometimes only to free their brothers. For some of our own men have taken Indians as prisoners. Right here, within the palisade, they force the

Indians to be their slaves. I would attack, too, if Caleb were held prisoner. And he would attack if I were held prisoner.

Tonight, clouds race across the moon. I hear an Indian drum like the beat of a huge heart. I hear whoops, as dismal as an owl calling.

Tonight, I feel afraid.

September 4, 1609

Oh, I can hardly contain myself. Oh, joy! This is what has happened. Captain Smith wishes to soothe things with the Indians. So in the morning, he will sail to the mouth of the river to their village. And I — Elizabeth Mary Barker — I shall go with him! He and Papa and Mama talked a long while yesterday afternoon. They think that the chief will find it pleasant to see another girl as young as his daughter Pocahontas. And since she has befriended us, I will go to befriend them. But this is sad — Jessie shall not go. She must stay and tend her mother. But I have promised to tell her every single thing. I cannot bring my journal, but I can remember every little thing. And I shall. I am so happy, I think I will not sleep at all tonight. To think that I shall go to a real Indian village. Who would have thought of such a thing?

September 5, 1609

This morning, when it was barely light, we sailed. Captain Smith, ten men — and me! We sailed the river through darkness, the trees hanging thick about us. My heart pounded wildly. I sat in the center of the canoe. I held tightly to the gift basket that Mama and the women had prepared. In it were beads and pins and shells. Captain Smith also brought gifts.

The sun was high when we arrived at the village. Never did I see such a scene! The village was alive with people and dogs. There were mat-covered houses, some round, some long. Fires burned in pits and children played — and oh, yes, there were dogs and creatures everywhere.

The elders and warriors welcomed the men. And the children and women swarmed about me. Some were brave and touched me. Some were shy and hid themselves. Some wanted to touch my skin, my hair, my skirts. I stood very still while they explored me. For I did not wish to frighten them.

One woman — no, she was little more than a girl — she had a baby strapped to her back. It was a tiny boy baby. And oh, looking at him, my heart did swell! He was just a few days old, his small head crowned with fine black hair. I wondered — is this what our baby will look like? I was so happy, I felt tears come to my eyes. A baby, a tiny, healthy baby.

And then, when the children had their fill, Pocahontas came to me. She led me to a roundhouse. I had to duck my head to fit inside. It was dusky like a cave, and cool, and smelled like the earth. I thought of our hot lean-tos. Could we learn to build such houses? And there, I sat on the ground. And Pocahontas gave me cool water to drink and corn cakes and venison. And oh, never have I had such a day of surprises and fun.

When it was time to leave, Captain Smith made promises to the Indians. And they made promises. Each promised to live with the other in peace.

Returning in the canoe, I carried gifts, too — a soft pair of deerskin moccasins, a beaded necklace, and a small woven basket. As we sailed home, I hugged the memories to me. I reminded myself of what I must tell Jessie. It seemed that all the way home my heart and mind sang happily.

September 6, 1609

Mistress Bolton has visions now. She is confused. She knows not where she is.

Jessie stayed by her side today.

September 7, 1609

Mistress Bolton died today. I cannot write more.

September 8, 1609

Mr. Bolton rubbed his dead wife's hands. It was as though he thought to bring her back to life. He has not stopped talking to her. But his voice is just a whisper now. I think he pleads with her to come back to life.

Jessie looked on.

I turned away. I did not know what to do.

September 8, later

I am filled up with sadness. Jessie does not cry. She does not speak. I asked Mama if she could have been struck dumb?

Mama says she will speak when she is able.

My heart hurts inside me.

September 9, 1609, midnight

We buried Mrs. Bolton tonight in the graveyard by the river. All of our burials are at night now. We do not wish the Indians to know how much sickness is here. They must believe that we are many. Reverend Harper said some prayers. We hurried back inside the palisade.

During these whole two days, Jessie has not spoken. She acts as though we are not here. After Jessie's mama was buried, Mr. Bolton did not speak. He just held Jessie tightly by her hand. My heart aches for them.

I am frightened for us all.

September 11, 1609

My hand shakes so I can barely hold my pen. My friend Claire is ill. She is delirious and hot with fever. Also, Jessie's papa fell ill.

And Mr. Foster, that dear man who cried to us about his children — he has died. Who will make the journey across the ocean? Who will bring the news to his children?

Two of the Bridger boys are also sick. I despise the Bridger boys, but I do not wish them ill. We have two or three deaths every day now.

Much of this day, I sat by Claire. I sang to her. I whispered tricks that Jessie and I will teach her when she is well.

I whispered to her, "Please do not die."

Today, even Papa grows silent and grim.

September 12, 1609

More bad news today. The men went to the storehouse where the supplies are kept for winter. They found little. The huge supplies are almost gone. Even the things we brought on ship — cheese, onions, biscuits, bacon, cloves, nutmeg, prunes, dates — most are gone.

At first, we thought our own men had been the thieves. But we found that the thieves were not men. The thieves were rats. They came aboard our ships. They disembarked with us.

Even Captain Smith looks tight and fearful this night. Gabriel Archer says this proves he should be in charge. As if he himself could stop those rats! But then, perhaps he could. He sneaks about like a rat himself.

September 13, 1609

Things do not stay grim for long with Papa here. He and Captain Smith have made this plan: Each day, each man must hunt for food. And each person must bring back as much food as Captain Smith brings back. If not, says Captain Smith, that person shall be locked outside the palisade gates. It sounds cruel. But it makes sense. For many do not pull their weight, like the Bridger boys. The ill ones are better. Still, not one of them works.

The rest of us begin to forage. We look for nuts and acorns, and herbs and fish. There are also deer and turkey. There are even those strange raccoons to eat. Also, Mr. Ratcliffe went up along the river and claims to have seen a bear. One large bear will see many people through the winter.

Papa tells me not to fear. Hard work and God will see us through.

I do believe in God. And in my papa. But in spite of that I am afraid.

September 14, 1609

Jessie's father is better. And Jessie smiled at me today. She spoke to me. Her eyes are sad, but Mama cares for her. Sometimes, I feel envy. It seems Mama is more tender with Jessie than with me. But I know Mama tries to ease Jessie's loss. I wonder what it is like to have no mother.

I will not think of it.

September 15, 1609

Jessie came with me today to search for food. Close in, the forest has been scavenged clear. So we go farther on. I do not mind. The Indians are not about, or perhaps they are. But they hide themselves well. They bother us not at all. We are too worried about food to worry about Indians right now.

Captain Smith is worried, though. The Indians are becoming more hostile. This is why: Rather than find food in the forest, some men have stolen the Indians' food. They have stolen the Indians' corn and robbed their gardens!

Captain Smith says his sympathy is with the Indians in this matter. He says they are badly treated by the wicked men here who want to spoil our good relations with the Indians.

It worries me much. Is it to be that neither

we of the settlement, nor the Indians, shall have food come winter?

September 16, 1609

I have made a new friend, Francis Collier. Who would have thought that a boy could be a friend? He has a funny mind and he is a wondrous story teller. All his stories are about food. He says he can taste food in his dreams.

I do not believe him. But he makes me laugh.

I think Francis and Caleb will be friends. When Caleb joins us here in the spring.

September 17, 1609

The men have built an open shed, a sick house. Each day, we women and children help there. Jessie and I give water to the sick ones. We lay wet cloths on their heads. Sometimes, we just hold their hands. Claire is no better. Her body is still hot with fever. And one of the twin girls, Sarah, lies ill. I sang to her today. She did not speak. She did not even open her eyes. But she knew I was there. I could tell because she squeezed my hand.

After a while, Francis Collier came and sat with me. He told Sarah a story — about food, of course. I listened closely so I could write it down. This is the story he told:

Once there was a strong young boy who met a girl in the forest. The little girl was sick. But the strong boy — his name was Francis — brought her cakes and scones. He brought a vat of butter as big around as a fat raccoon. He spread it on the scones. And the little girl, named Sarah, sat up and ate it. She got all well again. And on the morrow, she will get up from her bed.

That is how he told the story. Jessie and

I laughed. We thought perhaps Sarah smiled, too.

Abigail, her twin, laughed. She wanted her name put into the story. She will not leave her sister's side, though we tried to make her go. We fear the sickness will spread to her.

September 18, 1609

The whole fort is taken with madness. And I will tell you why. One of the new men has decided to go up the river to the falls. He will take many men to start a settlement there. He says that was part of the new charter with the Virginia Company. That charter was lost, though, on the *Sea Venture*!

Captain Smith sends them with his blessing. But I know he fears for their safety.

And then, more confusion! John Martin, another of the captains who thinks ill of

Captain Smith, said he, too, will take one hundred men. He means to go to the Nansemond territory. He wants to trade for food. Yet these men have stolen from the Indians and robbed their corn! They have continued to rob the Indians, even after our visit to the Indian village. I know that Captain Smith thinks them thieves and fools.

The men sailed away from our sight.

We wonder what will happen. We wonder how the Indians will greet them. We pray they come to no harm.

September 19, 1609

Such fun! Last night, Jessie slept in my lean-to, her bedroll beside my own. This is why: Yesterday, just as Mr. Martin was leaving, Jessie's father joined him. Papa tried to dissuade him. But Mr. Bolton was set on going. He said better to die at the hands of the Indians than to starve to death. He thinks lack of food caused his poor wife's death. He says he can bring back food for us. He promised to stay safe — as if anyone could promise that in this forest! Still, we count on his return.

So now, Jessie and I are really like sisters. Last night, we lay on our backs, holding hands. We looked up at millions of stars. It is almost as dark here as it was on board ship. But there was no creaking and swaying beneath us. And we did not bob up and down. We are a bit fearful, but not unhappy. We are together. A mockingbird sang in the new-fallen dark. And we whispered about the morrow.

September 20, 1609

Papa works furiously on our house. Jessie and I work alongside him. Mama still frowns, though, when I climb to the roof. And in the lean-to beside us, John Bridger lounges with his lazy brothers. They will be sorry when winter comes! But we will have our home ready. And we will be ready for our new baby. Mama's time will be soon, I know.

I pray to God to watch over her when that time comes.

September 21, 1609

Jessie and I have learned to walk as quietly as Indians. We practice on our tiptoes. Today, we tiptoed to spy on John Bridger. He sat on a rock, picking lice out of his head. From behind a tree, we sang out, Lousy head, lousy head! And then we ran like anything.

September 22, 1609

Something so bad. So terrible. I cannot write. Yet, write I must. Claire died last night. Little Sarah died today. Her twin, Abigail, lies near death herself. They are only four years old! They are babies. And Claire is nine years old like me.

Mama found me in the sick shed. I sat by the twins, holding their hands. I did not cry. I did not think I cried. Yet water ran out of my eyes and down my face. Mama took my hand and lifted me up. She held me close. She whispered, hush, hush.

But I cannot hush. And I cannot stop the crying.

September 22, almost dark

Tonight, I went to the river to think. It seemed as though God followed me there. So I talked to Him. I said, I am *furious* with You. Perhaps it is evil to speak so. But it is true what I did say. And I know He would not want me to lie. I said, I do not understand. Why do You let children die? And mothers and babies?

I said that I was scared.

I do not want to be motherless, like Jessie.

And then I began to cry. My tears have wet this page.

I am longing for Caleb and longing for spring. Yet spring is far away. For winter is not even upon us yet.

September 23, 1609

A little better today. Again, Pocahontas came to our settlement. She came at dawn, alone. She touched her left hand to her heart and raised her right hand to wave to Jessie and me. Then she went to Captain Smith.

For a long time they talked. Then Captain Smith called Papa to him. Pocahontas came to Jessie and me.

She beckoned to us and said, "See!" And she turned herself upside down, over and over like a tumbler. With her thin, deerskin leggings, her movements were free. Her legs flew into the air.

But Jessie and I wore skirts and shifts and petticoats.

Pocahontas tumbled again.

I looked at Jessie.

She looked at me.

We signaled to one another with our eyes. Then we signed to Pocahontas to follow us.

We ran to our secret place behind the well. We took off our skirts. We tied our petticoats to make breeches. And then, we turned ourselves upside down. We tumbled and tumbled. We tumbled until we were dizzy and fell on the ground.

I have not been so happy in a long time.

September 24, 1609

Such news! Captain Smith has called Papa to him. Papa is to be in charge while Captain Smith goes away. Captain Smith goes to see how the men have fared who sailed upriver to the falls. He is very worried about the Indians now. So now we will see if the men will obey Papa. We will see if Mr. Archer will stir up more trouble.

I feel sure that Papa will handle whatever might come.

September 25, 1609

I am weary of eating fish. And stewed vegetables. And fish. And stewed vegetables. Mama cooks it all in the big iron pot over the fire. Fish. And stewed vegetables. I think I would not mind if it tasted like fish. Or vegetables. But it tastes mostly like smoky fires and iron pots.

But at least it is food. So I am thankful. I think.

September 25, again

With Captain Smith gone, all is mostly well here. Mr. Archer has not been able to stir up trouble. But not because he does not try. Last night, he told Papa that perhaps we should feast on the food from the storehouse.

Papa just shook his head mildly. For I know Papa thinks about the coming winter.

Mr. Archer gave him an evil look and turned his back. He likely went to think up more mischief with his friend, George Percy. Most men, however, do not care just now about who is leader. They are more worried about food. And Indian attacks.

Last night, we heard hooting like owls. Yet most here say they are not owls, but warriors. We heard rumbles of drums upriver. Some here think that the Indians make ready to attack.

Jessie held my hand tightly tonight. I know she fears for her father. It would be too awful to have neither mother nor father in this world. I pray to God to keep Mr. Bolton safe.

September 26, 1609

We are less fearful today. Pocahontas again came to our town. She has taken Jessie and me as her special friends. We walk around, arm in arm. It is as though we are at home in England. With her bit of English, we can talk. She tells us names of plants. She helps us find the herbs that Mama needs. She tells us tales of the stars and moon. She gives a name to each wind that blows.

We play for hours. Even Mama does not tell me it is time for tasks. That is because many fear the nearby Indians might attack now. They surely know that Captain Smith is gone. But with Pocahontas here, we believe no harm will come to us.

Sometimes, I think I would like to be an Indian girl. How free and fearless she seems to be. Her voice is sweet and her laughter is merry.

Could it be that someday, we too will live free of want and fear?

September 26, nighttime

Mama was troubled today. Her eyes had a far-off look, and I saw her lip tremble.

I went to her and held her hand. She said it was Caleb. She misses him so. She said there is a hole in her heart. And oh, I know, I do. For there is a hole in my heart, too. But then Mama said, And to think we know nothing of how Caleb is. And he knows nothing of what happens here.

I knew I had to tell her. My heart pounded hard inside me, but I did, I told her. I said that I have been writing in a book for Caleb.

Mama smiled and nodded. She was not surprised. She already knew!

I waited for her to ask how I came to have

the book. But she did not ask. After a time, she touched my hair. Softly, she told me she was sure Caleb would not mind.

Oh, Mama, I cried. And I hugged her tight.

A big burden seems to have lifted from me tonight.

September 27, 1609

Such dreadful news! Captain Smith has returned. But he is injured! There was an explosion of gunpowder on his boat. He was badly burned. His pain was so severe, he leapt into the river. He almost drowned.

When he returned today, he called Papa to him. He told Papa even more bad news: It is true, what we feared. The Indians have been at war. They have killed many of our men who went to the falls.

So, even after Captain Smith was burned,

he went back. He did all he could to make peace with the Indians. For now, all is quiet. Our men are on their way back. But only some will return. Will Jessie's father return? We do not know. Tonight, Jessie was most silent. Inside my head, I said many, many prayers.

September 27, later

I must write two times in the same hour even though Mama calls me to my tasks. Jessie's papa has returned! He is silent though, and has been injured. One arm hangs limp by his side. He is in pain. But he has returned! He tells us to pray for the many who do not.

Also, Captain Smith suffers greatly. Mama treats him with aloe from the storehouse. She says she believes that he will live.

Captain Smith, too, says that he will live. I brought him fresh-dug clams today. He smiled at me. He told me that it would take more than gunpowder to kill John Smith!

And do you know what? I do believe that is the truth.

September 28, 1609

Something wonderful! Tonight will be our last night to lie out-of-doors. Our house is finished! The walls are up. There is a fireplace and a wondrous large chimney. Papa has daubed the chinks with mud. He even found enough glass at an abandoned glass house to make one window.

And I have helped to build this house!

We have not let Mama come inside to look. Not yet. First, Papa has hung a blanket in the middle. That is for Mama to be alone. It is the only thing I have heard Mama wish for — a private place. We brought in our bedding. We carried in the table we brought aboard our ship. We have three chairs that Papa has made here. We moved in the dishes and the iron cooking pot and Papa's tools. I brought in my chest with my clothes and my journal. Then, I gathered flowers. I put them in a jug. It is on the table inside the door. When Mama comes in, she will see a curtain for her private place. And flowers in our new house. I cannot wait.

September 29, 1609

Tonight, we moved into our house. Jessie came with us, for she is my sister now.

Mama stepped inside. She saw her curtain and her jug of flowers. Our house, our *home*, she said over and over. And then she began to cry!

At first, I was worried. But then I saw. She was not crying sad tears. She cried happy tears. She laughed, and hugged Papa. She hugged me and she hugged Jessie. They were strange hugs, for she could not get us close. Her belly is large now.

Papa smiled. And he, too, whispered, *Home*.

Home, I thought. But I could not say that word. For inside of me, I know it is not home. Not yet. It will not be home till Caleb comes. But it is *almost* a home.

September 30, 1609, early morning

A breeze blows in our open window and door. Outside, the birds are singing a morning song.

Inside, Mama and Papa sleep behind their curtain. Jessie sleeps beside me, her head pillowed on her arm. She looks peaceful in her sleep. She seems not so sad.

And I lie here and write. Now that Mama knows about my journal, I need not hide it.

This house is a good place. For now, almost-a-home is good indeed.

October 1, 1609

It is a worrisome time. Captain Smith must leave. He will return to England on one of the ships that arrived last month. His burns are severe. He cannot see to the work. He cannot calm the arguing. Captain Archer, with George Percy, is already taking control. And the men who have returned are terribly ill. Captain Smith is too sick to even go and see the Indians. And so, he must leave us.

My heart grieves. We shall miss him. We wonder what will happen without him here.

October 1, later

Jessie's papa has become grim and silent. He stares off into the woods. He has not added a single stick to his house. He is as idle as the Bridger boys. He looks about, shaking his head. It is as though his thoughts fly this way and that way. Jessie and I watch and worry.

We wonder if it is his injured arm that ails him.

October 2, 1609

I have a plan. I shall ask Captain Smith to visit Caleb when he returns to England. I believe he will do that. But Captain Smith has many important people around him. Somehow, I must find him alone. I want him to tell Caleb that all is well. And that I cannot wait to see him, come spring.

October 2, later

Captain Smith's ship is being prepared with what supplies can be spared. It has also been loaded with goods to take back to the Virginia Company. And here is something funny: Some men wanted to load the ship with gold. But there *is* no gold here. There is just earth with glints of yellow. Oh, how Captain Smith thundered, in spite of his weakness. He shouted that it was dirt! And he would not haul dirt to England!

Some men say it is pure gold. But we know it is pyrite — fool's gold.

So as usual — maybe for the last time — Captain Smith has had his way. His ship will sail on next Thursday. It will not haul dirt. It will sail with cedar wood and sassafras roots and furs. Wood takes up much room on board, but is needed in England.

We wish him Godspeed. But many of us feel sad. And frightened. Captain Smith will be sorely missed.

October 3, 1609

The days grow short. Winter, we know, will soon be here. Jessie's papa said it will be dreadful here come winter. But Jessie and I like the cool nights. Last evening, we dug deep into a pile of fallen leaves. We hid and spied on John Bridger. He was again scratching himself and picking at lice. But then I sneezed and blew leaves all over. John yelled and called us nasty, spying imps.

I thought that a nice compliment from John Bridger.

Later, when Jessie and I went to bed, I realized I miss sleeping out-of-doors. I miss the sky and the blanket of stars. I miss the breeze in the trees.

How odd, to miss such a thing. For in England, who would have thought to sleep outside?

I do believe one can become accustomed to most anything.

October 3, afternoon

Mama is restless. I think her time is almost here. She has been up since dawn. She walks back and forth. She goes out of our house to the village. She comes back in.

What kind of baby will Mama have? Jessie and I hope for a girl child.

I have the pincushion that we will give to Mama when the baby is born. I am spelling out a greeting with the pins. It says: *To Baby. Welcome to the world, the New World.* I do think that is a nice sentiment.

I believe Papa wishes for a son. I know that

in this land, a boy's strength is needed. Yet girls are just as strong as boys. I do know now that is the truth.

October 3, later

Today, Captain Smith called us to the Fort's open square. He was too weak to stand. But he sat on a tree stump to address us. Many men were knotted around him — those who wished to return to England with him. Captain Smith asked us to work with our new leader. He turned to Gabriel Archer who stood at his side. He turned to George Percy.

All of the men shook hands. For once, Mr. Archer's big fish mouth was quiet.

Watching, I thought: I do not like these men. But if they are to be our leaders, we will do as Captain Smith asks.

Then there was much to-do as men vied to

be chosen as crew. The Bridger family wishes to go. But Papa says that Captain Smith has already refused them. I know why — they would not work on board ship.

Captain Smith will choose his crew in the days left. I saw Mr. Collier at Captain Smith's side. I pray that Francis does not leave us!

October 5, 1609

I have just four days before Captain Smith leaves. I see him often, speaking quietly with Jessie's father and the other men. But I have not seen him alone.

When I asked Papa, he said, "What is your message, Elizabeth, my dear? I will take it for you."

I just shook my head. How could I say, I want him to visit Caleb? One must not ask important men to spend time on small matters.

Yet, inside of me, I know it is not a small matter.

It is a very large matter indeed, to me.

October 6, 1609

Mama's time has come. All night last night she paced. She picked up a flower. She put it down. She walked about. She lay on her pallet. She is pale and tired. Sometimes, she cries out with pain. She told me not to fear. This is the way of birthing, she said. When it is over we shall have a lovely baby. She smiled at me.

I tried to smile and tell her I know. But I do not know. Or could it be I know too much? So many babies and mamas have died in childbirth. But I have tucked the pincushion inside my apron. It is ready for Mama. And our baby, too.

October 6, later

It is taking a long time for this baby to be born. Two women are with Mama now, Mistress Collier and her sister, Mistress Whistler. Mistress Whistler is a silent old woman whom no one likes much. But they say she has experience with birthing. I worry and hope she indeed knows what she is doing.

Jessie and I have another worry — her papa. Tonight, in the dark, we saw him working silently. He was in his lean-to. He seemed to be taking things down — not raising them up! It is as if he has a great, dark secret.

October 6, night or is it morning, October 7?

It is taking too long! Mama cries and moans and cries out again. There are whispers from the women on the other side of the curtain.

Will Mama birth a dead baby? Or worse, will Mama die? Jessie knows my fear. She takes my hand and we sit outside. It is comforting to feel her hand. And to see the stars above our heads.

October 7, morning

The baby has still not been born. It is almost two days now. Papa said that it *will* happen. He said that Mama is being brave. Then he said, "You must be brave, too, Elizabeth. Babies can take a long, sweet time getting born."

He said it with a smile. But his face was grave. And he stayed beside our cabin this morning.

Jessie went with me to the riverbank. We sat together and stared into the water.

I think this makes her think of her own mama.

I think we are both tired of being brave.

October 7, later

Glory! A baby is born! Our baby, our brand-new baby. Mama is fine and well. Our baby is fine and well. And oh, Mama did not die. I was so afraid. A baby. A new beautiful baby. Mama laid her in my arms. . . . Oh, yes! I am so excited that she is here that I forgot to say — it is a girl. Her name will be Abigail.

I wanted to name her Americus. But Papa smiled and said we must save that name for a boy baby.

Abigail is beautiful. She is perfect. Her first cry was great and loud. And oh, I think that is the most beautiful sound I have heard in this land.

Papa keeps on smiling. Jessie and I laugh much. We gave Mama her gift. And when she read, *Welcome to the world, the New World —*

she cried! But I knew they were happy tears. She said it was the best gift ever.

Oh, to think — we have a tiny baby girl. She is already well-loved.

October 8, 1609

Baby Abigail continues to clamor loudly. She has a red, red face and a fierce little temper. When she wants to nurse, she howls. Sometimes, she howls even when she does not want to nurse. Last night, I took her outside. I showed her the stars. I told her of the things we would do together. For I am a big sister now. I turned her face up to see the moon. I told her the names of the winds as Pocahontas has told me. I told her about trees and raccoons and deer in the forest. I told her about Jessie. I told her about Francis Collier.

I especially told her about her brother, Caleb. She listened quietly a while. Then she began to howl again.

I touched her tiny mouth. She is a fierce little girl. I think she will do well in this new land.

October 8, later

Such news! I saw Captain Smith alone in the open place near the church. He called me to him. He said he wished to say good-bye.

And so I dared. I asked. I said, Oh, please, go see my brother.

And oh, my! Captain Smith put his hand on my shoulder. He told me that if God would bring him safely to England — then he would go see Caleb! That was his promise. He said it was his solemn promise.

October 8, night

I cannot bear it. I cannot bear this news. Mr. Bolton will return to England with Captain Smith. And Jessie, my friend, will go with him! She will go with him! How can I bear to have her leave?

But men are needed to man the ship. And with his skills and the way he works hard, Mr. Bolton will be useful. Their lean-to is already emptied out. He tells us we are fools to stay. He said those words to Papa. Oh, my heart is breaking this day.

Jessie and I sat at the river and held hands. We did not even talk. We wept.

October 8, later

Papa says there are many kinds of courage. Our courage will keep us here, he said. Mr. Bolton's courage will send them back to sea.

I do not have any courage.

Francis Collier came by to see baby Abigail. He says his family has chosen to stay and that makes me glad. But still, I cry. I do.

I cry.

October 9, 1609, morning

Just one more day Jessie and I will have together.

I think my heart will break. Almost time to sail and neither one of us can find a word to say. And me, I am the one who rushes on. I babble! Today, I have no words.

October 9, later

But oh, then more news! Life is up, and life is down. It is like the ocean in a hurricane. Mr. Bolton came to say good-bye. He promised Papa that he would go with Captain Smith to Caleb. He would tell him how we fare here. Then, just like that, my breath caught in my throat. I gasped and I blurted out words! I asked him to please take my journal to Caleb.

Mr. Bolton just stared at me. But Mama smiled and Papa, too. I do not know where that thought came from. It just flew into my head.

I asked again. I said that Caleb would then know how we fare here.

Mr. Bolton nodded. And he agreed. He did!

And then I thanked him again and again. I told him it was wonderful. Oh, it is. It is so wonderful!

I was so pleased, I babbled. Just as Mama tells me not to do. But I could be forgiven this time. So now, they will all go to Caleb — Captain Smith and Mr. Bolton — and Jessie! Jessie will go and meet my brother. I am so happy. I think my heart will fly right out of me.

Now, I hurry to finish writing here. So Caleb, my brother, my twin — so he shall know what has happened here.

October 9, as the sails are being unfurled

I sit at the dock, writing frantically. I have just these few moments.

Oh, Caleb, do you read now what is written here? I did not even tell about the ink. I ran out of English ink long ago. This ink is made of the juice of berries. I pray it holds and does not fade.

First, forgive me for taking your book. It was

wrong of me. But now you can know all that has happened to us. If the ink holds, then you know about baby Abigail. Just know that in spite of my worries and complaining here, all *is* well.

Mama and Papa and I — we are well. We are lonely. I am very lonely, for my dear friend Jessie is leaving me. Next to you, Caleb, she is my best friend in the whole world. But if you have this book, then you have met her. Oh, do you like her as well as I do? I believe you do, you must!

And Caleb, with each month's passing, you come closer to being with us. You will meet my friend, Francis Collier. You will meet the Indian men. You will like it here. Caleb, sometimes we are hungry. Ofttimes we are frightened. But we have a home here. Papa and I built it ourselves! And yes, I climbed the roof. I have done many things we did not think of doing in England. It is a small house. And I must admit, it smells a bit damp. It is different from England. But it is a house, Caleb, a home. It is our home. And it is beautiful to us.

Oh, Caleb, it is a lovely land. When you join us here come spring — we will rejoice.

For then it will be a real home indeed.

Home in America.

Historical Note

In 1607, the London Company in England sent an expedition to the Americas under the leadership of Captain Christopher Newport. The purpose was to settle there, in the hopes of finding goods and materials, and maybe even gold, to send back to England. On a warm spring day, the settlers landed on the Virginia coast, then sailed about thirty miles up the James River to the site of their new settlement, the first permanent one in the New World. Here they hung the flag of England. They hoped that by being far enough inland, they might be safe from the marauders and pirates who had been attacking other colonies.

Arrival at Jamestown.

This plan might have been a good one, but several things went very wrong. First, the land that they chose was poor for settling. It was in a wet marsh, full of mosquitoes that spread disease. Second, the land was inhabited by Indians who were wary of such strange visitors. But there were other problems, too, problems that the settlers brought with them from England. Some of the men who came on board the ships were lazy, and expected others to do their work. They did not know how to work hard. In addition, they had brought the wrong things—clothing that was too hot for this climate, foods that spoiled.

Some of the advertisements in England told how exciting life in America would be. Settlers came thinking they were headed for great adventure. Instead, they found hard times, hunger, disease, and trouble.

Relations with the Indians were unstable at times. And matters amongst the settlers also became tense. Eventually, a young colonist named John Smith took control of the colony and brought

An advertisement from England urging people to travel to Virginia.

some order to it. First, he made rules for the men there. One was "If you do not work, you do not eat!" Then, he worked at creating friendly, working relations with the Indians.

Captain John Smith.

He befriended Pocahontas, the daughter of the Indian chief Powhatan. The men traded with the Indians for food and necessary supplies. The Indians taught

Building a house at Jamestown.

Pocahontas leading John Smith through the woods.

the colonists how to plant corn, how to fish, and how to make canoes out of hollowed-out logs. All these things helped the colonists to survive, and even thrive, for a while.

When women and children came with more settlers in 1609, things were quiet at first. But soon there were more problems, mainly brought on by overcrowding and hunger, as the fort swelled with the newcomers. Also, the

Trading with Indians.

colonists and the Indians had become reckless in their relations with one another. Many people were killed in hostile, angry scuffles.

Then, in the fall of 1609, when Captain Smith was injured and had to return to England, things in the colony became much worse very quickly. Disease, discontent, and rivalry spread among the colonists. It was known as "The Starving Time," as hunger was their constant companion. The very survival of the colony was in doubt. When the next supply ship returned the following spring, only a few colonists were there to greet them. The rest had died of starvation or disease.

However, the arrival of those ships brought much needed food and supplies and many new people. The colony again began to thrive and soon, Jamestown was named the first capital of Virginia.

Women and children arriving at Jamestown.

About the Author

Writing about Jamestown, Virginia, enabled Patricia Hermes to work with some familiar material in a familiar setting. She says, "At one time, I lived in Tidewater, Virginia, just a few miles from the original Jamestown settlement. I remember how hot and humid the summers were there. I know about the bugs. I know about the winter cold. I know about the swaying pines and the whisper of the rivers and the sandy soil and the rich marshland alive with birds.

"I also remember how lonely I first felt when I moved there. So, when I created Elizabeth and her twin brother, Caleb, I think I knew something of how she felt. I knew how hard it is to leave family and friends. I knew how scary it was to be in a strange place with strange people and new foods, and different customs. I knew how lonesome it could be."

Patricia Hermes is the author of over thirty books for children and young adults, including *Mama, Let's Dance*; *You Shouldn't Have to Say Goodbye*; *Cheat the Moon*; and *Kevin Corbett Eats Flies*. Many of her award-winning books were named ALA Best Books or received the IRA-CBC Children's Choice Award.

Acknowledgments

Grateful acknowledgment is made for permission to reprint the following:

Cover portrait and frontispiece by Glenn Harrington.

Page 100: The arrival of the first English colonists at Jamestown, Virginia, wood engraving, American, nineteenth century, The Granger Collection, New York, New York.

Page 101: Advertisement, Charlotte Engraving Co., Charlotte, North Carolina.

Page 102 (top): Captain John Smith, line engraving, detail from Smith's map of Virginia, 1616, The Granger Collection, New York, New York.

Page 102 (bottom): Building a house at Jamestown, wood engraving, nineteenth century, ibid.

Page 103: Pocahontas brings corn to the colonists at Jamestown, wood engraving, American, nineteenth century, ibid.

Page 104: Trading with Indians, North Wind Picture Archives, Alfred, Maine.

Page 105: Wives of the settlers at Jamestown, Library of Congress.

For Jessica Camille Hermes

※

While the events described and some of the characters in this book may be based on actual historical events and real people, Elizabeth Barker is a fictional character, created by the author, and her diary is a work of fiction.

Copyright © 2000 by Patricia Hermes

All rights reserved. Published by Scholastic Inc.
555 Broadway, New York, New York 10012.
SCHOLASTIC, MY AMERICA, and associated logos are trademarks of Scholastic Inc.

No part of this publication may be reproduced, or stored in a retrieval system, or transmitted in any form or by any means, electronic, mechanical, photocopying, recording, or otherwise, without the written permission of the publisher.
For information regarding permission, write to Scholastic Inc., Attention: Permissions Department, 555 Broadway, New York, New York 10012.

Library of Congress Cataloging-in-Publication Data
Hermes, Patricia.
Our strange new land: Elizabeth's diary, Jamestown, Virginia, 1609.
p. cm. — (My America)
Includes bibliographical references
Summary: Nine-year-old Elizabeth keeps a journal of her experiences in the New World as she encounters Indians, suffers hunger and the death of friends, and helps her father build their first home.
ISBN 0-439-11208-7
1. Jamestown (Va.). — History — Juvenile fiction.
2. Virginia — History — Colonial period, ca. 1600–1775 — Juvenile fiction.
[1. Jamestown (Va.) — History — Fiction.
2. Virginia — History — Colonial period, ca. 1600–1775 — Fiction. 3. Diaries — Fiction.]
I. Title. II. Series.
PZ7.H4317Ou 2000
[Fic] — dc21   99-056356
CIP AC

10 9 8 7 6 5 4 3 2   0/0 01 02 03 04 05

Photo research by Zoe Moffitt
Book design by Elizabeth B. Parisi
Printed in the U.S.A.
First edition, June 2000

※